SNAP

Alison McGhee is the author of three critically acclaimed novels for adults: *Rainlight, Was It Beautiful?* and *Shadow Baby.* She is also the author of a picture book, *Countdown to Kindergarten,* illustrated by Harry Bliss. She says, "Recently I went through a rubber band phase, in which I wore several on my wrist at all times and snapped them in an effort to retrain myself out of a couple of bad habits. Sadly, the bad habits remained — but happily, *Snap* was born." Alison McGhee lives in Minnesota, USA.

SNAP

a novel

Alison McGhee

WALKER BOOKS
AND SUBSIDIARIES

LONDON · BOSTON · SYDNEY · AUCKLAND

This is a work of fiction. Names, characters, places and
incidents are either the product of the author's imagination
or, if real, are used fictitiously.

First published 2004 by Walker Books Ltd
87 Vauxhall Walk, London SE11 5HJ

2 4 6 8 10 9 7 5 3 1

Text © 2004 Alison McGhee
Cover photograph © 2004 Christine Rodin

The right of Alison McGhee to be identified as author
of this work has been asserted by her in accordance with
the Copyright, Designs and Patents Act 1988

This book has been typeset in Horley Old Style and OPTICookeSans

Printed in Great Britain by J.H. Haynes & Co. Ltd

British Library Cataloguing in Publication Data:
a catalogue record for this book
is available from the British Library

ISBN 0-7445-9380-8

www.walkerbooks.co.uk

To Luke O'Brien

 *One*

I, Edwina Beckey, am a girl of lists.

I love lists of all kinds: to-do lists, grocery lists, homework lists, New Year's resolutions, books read, books to be read, best friends, next-best friends, favorite names, favorite nick-names, favorite movies, favorite foods, favorite you name it. If more people made lists, the world would be more predictable and less chaotic.

That's not to say that I myself am an organized person. Take my school desk, for example.

Wouldn't you think that, being a girl of lists, my school desktop could be lifted to reveal perfectly organized piles of books, notebooks, erasers, pens, pencils, and markers?

Not so.

My school desk is a mess. So is my desk at home. So are my bureau and my closet. I aspire to neatness and organization, but despite my list making, I have not yet attained it.

Here I am, in simple list form:

Name: Edwina Stiles Beckey.
Nickname: Eddie.
Home: North Sterns, New York, in the
    foothills of the Adirondack Mountains.
Family: Mother, Mildred. Father, Keith.
Grade: Just passed sixth, heading into
    seventh.
Pets: Hamster (deceased). Goldfish (three;
    deceased). Raccoon (deceased).
    Caterpillar (turned self into a butterfly).

Favorite season: Autumn.
Favorite color: Pine trees in winter.
Best friend: Sally Hobart.

I love not only lists but all listlike arrays of objects, such as rows of rubber bands. I have six of them, in all different colors, on my left wrist, to be snapped when necessary.

1. **The red one:** storing food in my cheeks when I eat.

"Eddie, sweetie, you're not a chipmunk," my father once said. "We have plenty of provisions to get you through the winter."

2. **The blue one:** thinking of my best friend Sally Hobart's grandmother as Willie instead of as Sally's grandmother. Sally's grandmother loves to walk. She walks to Sterns and back almost every day from the house where she lives with Sally, up here in North Sterns, in the foothills of the Adirondack Mountains, which is how Sally and I like to refer to our home.

Sally's grandmother carries a green pail in one hand and a stick in the other, and she swings her arms. Sometimes she sings. As we pass by on the school bus, she waves the pail and the stick back and forth over her head and shouts out our names, mine and Sally's.

But Sally's grandmother said to me recently, "My name is Willie, did you know that?"

I realized right in that moment that I had never called Sally's grandmother by name, any kind of name. I had never said, "Mrs. Hobart," or "Grandma Hobart," or even "Hey." And there was something in her voice, something that made me think she wanted to be called Willie.

So I added the blue rubber band to my wrist.

3. **The yellow one:** tipping back in chairs.

Sally and I like tipping back in chairs, but it hurts Sally's grandmother — *Willie* — to see us do it. That's because Willie's childhood friend Sara tipped back too far in a chair the day she graduated from high school, and broke her neck and died. Every time Willie sees someone tipping back in a chair, she tells that person about Sara, about the navy blue velvet dress she was wearing and how fast it all happened.

When I see Sally tipping back in a chair, I give her a meaningful look and snap my yellow rubber band. But she just laughs and tips back farther.

4. The white one: covering my mouth when I laugh.

Once, at a restaurant in Utica with my parents, I saw a girl with short hair and slightly long bangs. She covered her mouth with her hand when she laughed, and since she seemed to laugh all the time, her hand was constantly covering her mouth. It annoyed me, the sight of this girl constantly laughing with her hand over her mouth. She was irritating. Then I realized that it was one of those restaurants with a mirror running all along the opposite wall, so that what you think is a whole other room is actually just the reflection of the room you yourself are sitting in.

The irritating girl was me.

5. **The pink one:** whistling under my breath so that it drives other people crazy.

I'm not a good whistler. What I call a whistle is a mutant form of whistling that sounds like the faintest recorder in the world playing itself out of tune. That's what Sally told me once, anyway.

There's another rubber band too.

6. **Purple.** It's the one highest on my forearm. It hurts the most when it's snapped. What I tell people, if they ask, is that my purple rubber band stands for "Remember to wear your glasses." When I put my glasses on, the world is sharp-edged and bright. When teachers ask why I'm not wearing my glasses, I tell them that I just forgot to, which is sometimes true but sometimes not. Most people don't know that a little fuzziness isn't always a bad thing.

There's another reason why I keep the purple band on my wrist. But that reason, I don't talk about.

 *Two*

Sally Hobart is my best friend.

Here is a partial list of what I know about Sally:

Name: Sally Wilmarth Hobart.
Favorite smell: Wood smoke.
Favorite kind of cheese: Limburger.
Favorite season: Spring.
Favorite color: White.
Best friend: Eddie Beckey.

Favorite food: Chocolate-covered sprinkle doughnuts from the bakery at the back of Jewell's Groceries.

I know so much else about Sally: her favorite books, the contents of her locker, the fact that on cheese pizza day she will buy, instead of bring, her lunch. Her preferred Monopoly piece, the only piece she will play with? The dog, because she's always wanted one.

She used to suck her thumb but forced herself to stop.

Her favorite class is earth science.

Favorite body of water? The meander that twists its way through the meadow below her house.

Favorite place in the world? The Cabin, where every summer we go camping.

I could make a list of everything I know about Sally. But I wouldn't because Sally says that my lists are "spontaneity crushers."

* * *

Willie says that Sally is a sugar fiend.

"Sally," Willie says, "consider the cave children. Did they wake up in the morning craving chocolate-covered sprinkle doughnuts?"

"Cave children probably ate bloody chunks of raw meat for breakfast," Sally says. "And they lived in caves. I'd rather live in a house and eat sprinkle doughnuts."

Willie thinks of herself as an anti-sugarist.

Given a choice between salty and sweet, Sally's grandmother — *Willie* — will choose salty every time. That's why she prefers crackers over cookies. She bakes them herself. She rolls the cracker dough out thin on a cookie sheet and pricks it all over with a fork. After the dough is baked, when it's brown and cool, she breaks it into pieces. She bakes all kinds of crackers: cracked-pepper Parmesan, plain soda, Vermont cheddar with maple syrup. Sometimes I look up cracker recipes in the library so as to test her with the names of weird ones. Crackers I had never even imagined the existence of, Sally's grandmother knows all about.

But still, she buys sprinkle doughnuts for Sally.

"One of these days I'm going to stop and buy chunks of raw meat instead so that you can work on your cave-girl technique," she says. "You just watch."

She's been saying that for years.

What Sally loves most: Willie.
What Willie loves most: Sally.

I once would have thought there was nothing I didn't know about my best friend, but on the last day of sixth grade, that changed. Sally and I were riding the bus home to North Sterns, out here on the Remsen border, where the foothills rise up purple and shadowy, and it came to me that I hadn't seen Sally's grandmother for a while. Where was she? Why was she not tromping her way south along Route 274, scissoring both her arms at us to say hello as we passed her? Where was she, Willie, with her green pail and her keep-away-the-dogs stick?

I realized that I had not been to dinner at Sally's house in a while. I could see the red-and-white checked tablecloth that Willie spreads in my honor, and I could smell the spaghetti sauce she makes for us, her hours-long spaghetti sauce whose secret ingredient is V8 juice — yes, V8 — bubbling away on the stove.

"Sally? Where's your grandmother?"

Sally was next to me on the long green vinyl seat of the bus, eight seats behind Shari, the driver. Sally had opened up her lunch box and was eating the apple she hadn't eaten at lunch. She usually saves something for the bus ride. It's a long one, especially the way Shari drives. You would think, looking at her, that Shari would drive fast and curse a lot, but no.

"Sally?"

Sally munched on.

"Is she sick?"

"She's fine," Sally said, around her mouthful of apple.

"Why isn't she out walking, then?"

Sally sat there next to me on the green vinyl seat, crunching away on that apple. She didn't look at me. Something flitted through me, a shadow of a feeling that made my stomach flutter. I gazed out the bus window and willed Willie to appear. I willed her arms to be up in the air, waving her hello to us. I willed her to be around the next curve, her big smile and her green pail. She wasn't.

Sally didn't say anything. I felt for my purple rubber band.

Snap.

Three

In the woods behind the Cabin, a blue bicycle hangs in a tree. As far as I know, only two people here in Sterns know about the blue bicycle, and those two people are Sally and me. We discovered it by accident one day when we were seven, which according to Sally's grandmother — *Willie* — is the age of reason.

"So," Willie said. "Seven."

It was July, the summer after second grade. Sally and I were born in July. We were standing in her kitchen.

"Seven," Willie said again. "The age of reason. Has the world unfolded itself to you in all its mystery and power, and do you now understand your purpose in it?"

Sally and I looked at each other, then back at Willie. We nodded.

But we had no idea what she was talking about.

"Excellent," she said. "Have a cracker."

We ate our crackers and went out to the woods near the Cabin. Maples and oaks, mostly, with a few butternuts here and there. That day, we went farther than we had ever gone before, into what felt like deep woods.

It was Sally who saw it first. She pointed, and my eyes followed her pointing finger.

"Is that a bicycle?" I said.

Sally lowered her finger.

"Yes, it is," I answered myself. "It's a blue bicycle."

We stood there shading our eyes against the sun and staring up at that maple tree, the maple tree where a blue bicycle hung suspended, its frame and one tire wrapped around — grown into — the branches. The blue bicycle had been in that tree for a long time. Even at seven we knew enough to know that.

We weren't old enough yet to wonder about how it got there in the first place, who had brought a blue bicycle into these forgotten woods, or why. We just stood and looked up in the tree, high up where the bicycle hung, one wheel twirling slowly in the breeze, so slowly that the sunlight sparkling off its rusty chrome seemed like a mirage.

Whose bicycle was it?

Sometimes I wonder about that. It's the same kind of bicycle that Sally and I used to ride when we were seven and eight and nine, when I would keep lists that tracked our speed and distance using the speedometers that Willie bought us.

Fastest downhill: William T. Jones's hill:
  35 mph on a very windy day two years
  ago, a speed we have never been able to
  replicate.
Distance from Sally's house to mine the
  short way: 2.1 miles.
Distance from Sally's house to mine the
  long way: 3.4 miles.

You can lean your head back, and shade your eyes if it's a sunny day, and gaze up to the top of that gigantic maple, and there the bicycle will be. Rusting in spots; shining in others. On windy days, when the slender branches near the top of the maple toss and turn, one wheel of the bicycle spins. It looks lazy, that wheel, as if it knows that its purpose in life used to be to get places and go somewhere, but now all it has is air to turn against.

I used to think that nothing much would ever change from the way it was. But the first day of summer, the first *hour* of summer, as

I was walking by myself in the bicycle woods in search of double acorns to add to my double-acorn collection, I glanced up to my left to see how the bicycle was doing.

And it was no longer a bicycle.

What used to be a blue bicycle had become encircled and covered over by the limbs of the tree. The blue bicycle is no longer itself. Is that the way it is with everything? Is everything in this world changing all the time, in little ways, ways I can't even see?

Sally's grandmother — *Willie* — changed, and I never saw it coming. The first inkling I had was that last day of school, on the bus, when Sally wouldn't look at me or answer my questions.

Willie has carried a green pail by her side for as long as I've known her. No purse for her. Pail in hand, Willie walks the five miles into Sterns come sleet, come hail, come rain, come snow.

The way Willie walks is the way a person who has walked her entire life walks. She gulps up the road. Her pail goes into Sterns empty and comes back with a loaf of bread sticking out of it. A roll of stamps. A library book or three or four for Sally. Red and orange maple leaves, I saw piled in there once, bright against the green of the plastic pail. Next time I went to their house, those leaves had been pressed between wax paper and were hanging in the kitchen window to catch the sun.

As long as I can remember, Willie has gotten up early on Sunday morning and walked into Sterns. She brings back chocolate-covered sprinkle doughnuts. She sits at the kitchen table with us. We eat the doughnuts and Willie watches us, her voice a small waterfall of words and laughter. This has been our routine for years.

"Don't you want a doughnut?" I asked her once, way in the beginning, before I knew how she felt about sugar.

"Thank you, Eddie, but unlike my grand-daughter, I'm not much of a sugar person," she said. "I do love a good doughnut hole, though."

She reached over to my doughnut and pretended to pluck out the hole, which because it was a hole was already gone. And she ate it. I watched her as she rolled her eyes and smiled and pretended to chew.

"Heavenly," she said. "Indescribably, existentially delicious."

And I could almost taste that hole myself, even though a hole is by definition nonexistent. I could almost feel it filling my mouth with its indescribably, existentially delicious flavor.

Until now, nothing about Willie had ever changed, her walking, her green pail, her buying of sprinkle doughnuts for Sally, the way she spread a red-and-white checked tablecloth on the kitchen table whenever I went to their house. But none of this had happened lately. Sunday mornings have come and gone, and there have been no sprinkle doughnuts.

I never thought about it, but if I had, I would have assumed that Willie would stay the same forever, and Sally would live with her, here in Sterns, in the foothills of the Adirondacks, until Sally was grown-up and had a job and a house and maybe a dog even, the dog she's always wanted.

 *Four*

Sally's and my Cabin is down the hill past the cornfield, through the woods behind Sally's house, where she lives with her grandmother. Not everyone calls the Cabin a cabin.

> *What my mother calls it:* A shack.
> *What Sophie, waitress at Queen of the*
> *Frosties, calls it:* A hut.
> *What Sally's grandmother — Willie —*
> *calls it:* A hovel.

The first time Sally and I told Willie that we wanted to go camping at the Cabin by ourselves, she headed down there with her keep-away-the-dogs stick. She poked and jabbed at the Cabin, inside and out. She had to bend down to get through the doorway, and Sally's grandmother — *Willie* — is not a tall woman.

"This used to be a chicken coop," she said. "Did you know that?"

She put both hands against the falling-down roof and shoved with all her strength. The Cabin swayed but it did not fall. Willie dusted off her hands and squinted.

"Well, it's far removed from the halcyon days of its chicken coop youth," she said. "But I guess it's not likely to fall down on your heads while you lie sleeping."

That was how Willie gave us her permission.

Sally and I have a pact that when camping at the Cabin, we head into the wilderness with our doubled-up grocery bags of supplies and live off the land. No returns to her house or mine are allowed.

And no lists prior to packing.

"You make too many lists," Sally says. "There should be one area of Eddie life that is list free, and I decree that area to be the Cabin."

I wanted to go camping the first weekend that school was out.

"Let's go," I said to Sally.

We were sitting on the front step of her house, the front step that has both our hand-prints in one corner. The day the concrete was poured, Willie had called us out to render our handprints immortal. That was the way she put it.

"Let's go this weekend," I said.

No answer.

"It'd be so much fun," I said. "The roaring fire, the smell of wood smoke. The s'mores."

No answer.

Sally sat next to me with two sticks in her lap. Twigs on the ground in front of her formed a sort of cone shape. Beneath them she had piled some pine needles and a few old leaves that didn't look very dry. Her entire life Sally has wanted to start a fire by rubbing two sticks together. It's one of her dreams.

"What do you say? Camping at the Cabin this weekend?"

No answer.

"Imagine a nicely toasted marshmallow," I said, "a soft chocolate bar, and a crisp graham cracker."

No answer.

"I dream of s'mores."

"I don't," Sally said. "Not anymore."

"What?"

"I don't dream of s'mores," Sally said. "They're too sweet."

"Did you just say something is too sweet?"

"Yes."

"Since when?"

"Since right now."

"You've got to be kidding me," I said. "What about ice cream? What about brown sugar on oatmeal? What about blueberry pie?"

No answer. It was late in the afternoon. To the west the sun was sinking below the rounded humps of the Adirondacks. Sally rubbed her sticks together furiously.

"Are you saying you've become an anti-sugarist?" I said.

"Sugar's bad for you."

"But what about chocolate-covered sprinkle doughnuts?"

"I will never eat another chocolate-covered sprinkle doughnut," Sally said.

She tossed her sticks into the grass and went up on the porch to get her jump rope. She went out to the dirt jump-rope patch under the maple and started practicing her Rope Power routine: cancan, double under, grapevine.

 *Five*

Up until I was eight or nine, well past the age of reason, I used to think that Sally lived with her grandmother because Jill, her mother, doesn't talk. Maybe I assumed that children weren't allowed to live with their mothers if their mothers didn't talk. Then one day it dawned on me that other parents — blind parents, deaf parents, parents who don't have any legs or any arms — still live with their children.

Sally's mother's name is Jill. She lives in Remsen, in an apartment next to the blacksmith. She works in Remsen too, at BJ's Foods. Jill's checkout lane is lane 3, and when I was little, I always told my mother to go to lane 3 if Jill was working there. Lollipops is why. She had a small cardboard box filled with them: grape, lime, orange, lemon, and cherry. After she finished checking and bagging the groceries, she would pull out the little box and hold it up in the air, looking at my mother with a questioning look.

"Please, Mom?" I used to say. "Please?"

My mother used to nod, and then Jill would lower the box to my height, so that I could see into it and pick. Lime, that was my favorite. And it must not have been any other kid's favorite, because there were always plenty of green lollipops to choose from.

"What do you say?" my mother used to say.

"Thank you, Jill," I would say back.

Most people would have said, "You're welcome," back to me. "Thank you" calls for "you're welcome." But not Jill. Jill doesn't talk.

Perhaps Sally and Willie also chose lane 3 so as to see Jill. Perhaps Sally used to say hello to her mother, years ago, before the age of reason. Had her mother ever said hello back? Had her mother ever held out the box of lollipops to Sally?

"Jill was very young when she had Sally," my mother told me when I asked her about the situation.

"How young is very young?"

"Fifteen, I think."

When you're fifteen, you're still in high school. You haven't even reached your full height when you're fifteen. You have a couple years of growing left.

"Jill wasn't able to take care of Sally by herself," my mother said.

"Is that because she doesn't talk?"

"No," my mother said. "Or maybe it is, in a way. Things have always been hard for Jill. Jill doesn't seem equipped for the world."

Sometimes I wonder if Sally misses the sound of her mother's voice. Sometimes I wonder if she ever even heard her mother's voice. If you've never heard something, like the sound of your mother's voice, would you miss it anyway?

"Wilhelmina was very strong," my mother said. "I don't recall her ever saying one chastising word about the situation. She just took over and made a good life for Sally."

Wilhelmina is Willie's proper name, although everyone except my mother calls her Willie. But my mother believes in full names, which is why she calls me Edwina and why she goes only by Mildred. It's not a common name these days, Mildred. Some might even say that it's an ugly name. But my mother is not ugly. My mother, were she being born today, wouldn't be named Mildred. She would be named Ashley, maybe, or Gillian, or Samantha. Does she care? No.

"It's my God-given name" is what she says,

"and my God-given name is what I want to be called."

Even my father, who loves her to the ends of the earth, calls her Mildred. My mother is a nicknameless person to everyone but me. I call her Mom.

Six

Sometimes Sally and I play a game we call Blind. One of us closes her eyes — squinches them shut so that no light comes in — and the other takes her arm and leads her around. "Come on," we say to each other, "it's all right." At first it feels wrong, walking around with my eyes closed. But after a while I focus on Sally's arm and her voice. "Mud puddle coming up," she'll say. "Step to your right." Or "Rock straight ahead; follow my lead."

Sometimes she'll slip something into my hand, a cellophane-wrapped mint from the basket at the Café Nero cash register, for example, or a leaf. "Tell me what kind of leaf this is," she'll say. "No peeking allowed."

I'm good at figuring out what the things she gives me are. Leaves especially; maple leaves most especially. If you play Blind often enough, your fingers get used to sensing what something really is, its true shape.

Sometimes Sally and I jump rope blind. You can't think about it too much or you'll get stuck. You just have to close your eyes and begin.

Sally, who's on the Rope Power team at school, practices all her tricks blind: rocker rebound forwards, crisscrosses, bleakings, and double unders. I've watched her go from not being able to do a double rebound forward, which is the easiest of all Rope Power tricks, to doing a crisscross, which is not so easy, to a backward crisscross, which is hard, to a three-sixty, which is harder. I've seen her land a cancan, and I watch her now, working on a grape-vine, which is the final and most difficult Rope Power trick. And she does them all blind. Sally is known at school as an expert rope-jumper.

"You can't think about it," she says. "That's the key."

Few people know this about Sally, but when we were very young, she used to be scared to jump rope. We were at my house doing dares: eat this lump of Play-Doh, eat this spoonful of nutmeg, eat this, eat that. Then we moved into physical dares. Leap from the recliner to the couch! Jump from the fourth stair to the bottom!

"Jump, Sally!" was what I remember saying that day that we were daring each other.

But she couldn't. She couldn't jump at all. That was something I didn't know about Sally back then, how scared she was to jump over anything. Finally I coiled up my jump rope, my rainbow-colored rope with red plastic handles, and lessened the dare to just that: jump over the jump rope, lying on the rug in a little coiled lump. She looked down at the rope at her feet, curvy and still like a snake sleeping in the sun, and she started to cry.

"I can't," she said.

Her hair was short then, the same dark brown it is now, and Willie had put a purple barrette in it that day. The purple was barely visible against the darkness of her hair, but there was a row of tiny rhinestones on the clasp, and when her head moved, the rhinestones caught the light and winked. She was crying, and I remember how strange it seemed that she could be so sad and so beautiful at the same time, with the sunlight striking and sparking off her dark head the way it did that day.

She couldn't see how beautiful she looked, but I could. You'll never be able to see your own face. Have you ever thought about that? When you're looking in the mirror, you're not seeing your own face in real life. You're seeing a reflection. The backward image of yourself.

I never thought about this until I caught sight of my own reflection in that restaurant in Utica. It was then that I saw how I covered my mouth when I laugh, and what an irritating habit it was.

Even though I'm not always aware of covering my mouth when I laugh, I snap my white rubber band often, just for good measure.

 *Seven*

"Edwina, please don't store food in your cheeks," my mother said.

My mother and I were eating supper from paper plates while sitting around the kitchen table, an indoor semi-picnic. It was one of the weeks, which are every other week, when my father was on the road. He's a salesman. It was early summer and the windows were wide open. Bumblebees kept buzzing up against the screens.

I snapped my red rubber band.

"My daughter, the chipmunk," my mother said. "Swallow."

I swallowed. My wrist stung.

"Edwina, please don't tip back in your chair," my mother said.

I snapped my yellow rubber band. My wrist stung worse.

"You sound like Sally's grandmother," I said.

"I do? In what way?"

"'Never tip back in a chair,'" I recited, "'because you might end up like my friend Sara on the day we graduated from high school.'"

"Which is how?"

"Dead."

"Oh," my mother said. "My."

She reached up to the cupboard above the stove, the cupboard where the hammer and nails are kept, and she pulled down a glass baby-food jar filled with eight-penny nails.

"Mom, is Willie all right?"

Red flag. I could see it immediately. My mother's back stiffened. I waited for her to set the jar on the counter. I knew that she would answer me. She always does. She's never lied to me, my mother.

She turned and faced me. Her fingers were still gripped over the top of the eight-penny nail baby-food jar. She looked right at me.

"Mom? Is Willie all right?"

"No."

I waited. She was still looking at me. I had the feeling that my mother wanted to lie to me. That if she could've, she would've.

"What's wrong with her?"

"She's sick."

"What kind of sickness?"

"She has a disease that's harming her blood."

"Will she get better?"

"No."

I waited then. I waited for my mother to tell me something that would take away the way the word *no* sounded, hanging in the air of the kitchen the way it did. There must be something she could say that would take away the sound of that word, and I waited for her to say it.

"She won't?"

That's what I finally said.

My mother shook her head. Her eyes darkened the way they sometimes do, the way they do when she has to do something she doesn't want to do.

"I'm sorry," she said.

That was all she said.

"Are you sure?" I said. "Because Sally's only eleven."

My mother nodded. She knew exactly what I was talking about, Sally and her elevenness. She stood there in the kitchen, with the little jar of eight-penny nails behind her, nodding. In my mind I could see Willie sitting with us at her kitchen table, eating her way through a stack of doughnut holes while Sally sat laughing on her lap, half a sprinkle doughnut in each hand.

"She needs her grandmother," I said. "She *needs* her."

My mother kept nodding.

I started snapping my purple rubber band. My mother stood there for a long time, and I sat there snapping, and the fluorescent light above our heads was semi-blue and after a while I could hear its faint buzzing.

 *Eight*

Sometimes, in school or riding the school bus or in the grocery store or walking the two sidewalks of Sterns, here where I live in the foothills of the Adirondacks, I look at the girls passing by and think, *Who did her hair?*

I notice hair. The hair I want is hair like Sally's, long curly hair that swoops over my shoulders and down my back. My own hair is colorless — not-brown, not-blond — and grows slower than anyone else's I know. Last Thanksgiving I decided to grow my bangs out.

"Oh, you're growing out your bangs?"

I looked forward to having my friends ask me that question. There's a certain way that girls ask that question of someone who has straight hair and is in a bangs-growing stage. They tilt their head a bit; they nod knowingly. Everyone knows what it's like. It's a difficult thing.

But I looked forward to it. I looked forward to the day when I would be able to sigh and roll my eyes and pull dramatically on my used-to-be-bangs.

And I'm still looking forward to that day.

Because my bangs have still not grown out enough to have a single person tilt her head and ask me sympathetically, "You're growing out your bangs?"

My hair has not even needed to be trimmed.

Unlike Sally's hair, long and dark brown with red that glows when the sun is shining on her head. Left undone, Sally's hair rises around her head like a halo in the sunshine. When she jumps rope, her undone hair floats behind her, bouncing in rhythm to her strides. When Sally is in the haymow and the sun is shining through the unpaned window, dust motes rise around her haloed head.

The first day I met Sally, which was the first day of second grade, in Mrs. Lattimore's class, the sun shone and sparkled on her hair. I looked at her long braids, glinting red and brown, and wondered if she had done them herself. I had been growing out my own hair all summer, but it grew so slowly that even I couldn't tell the difference. Sally had the hair I had always wanted.

Sally had just transferred from Remsen Elementary, the next school north. There she was, with her long auburn braids, holding her grandmother's hand. Our names were Magic Markered in uppercase, big and black and bold, on scissored rectangles of masking tape affixed to one of the tables near the back of the classroom.

SALLY HOBART

And me, also in uppercase black:

EDWINA BECKEY

Next to our table were (1) stacked plastic storage boxes filled with markers, crayons, colored pencils, glue sticks, scissors, stencils, and colored pipe cleaners, (2) the bathroom with its open door, low toilet, and low sink, (3) a long row of hooks, large ones for coats, smaller ones for backpacks, (4) a row of cubbies, each with an orange construction-paper nametag leaf taped to it, each holding a newly sharpened pencil, and (5) a cage holding what at that point I did not know was a hedgehog.

All I knew was what the animal I was staring at wasn't: a cat, a raccoon, a ferret like the kind I remembered seeing in a pet shop, a rat, a donkey, an elephant, a giraffe. At that point the hedgehog was just a nameless semi-porcupinelike animal.

That's because I was a second grader, lacking knowledge. Second graders are just a few years out of toddlerhood, when you think about it. The age of seven is known as the age of reason, but for most seven-year-olds reason has yet to come.

Mrs. Lattimore spoke softly, but the way she shook her head when her black curls got into her eyes made me tense.

"Any questions so far?"

I raised my hand. I wanted to know what was in that cage.

"Yes, Edwina?"

"Eddie," I said.

She raised her eyebrows. "Eddie is your nickname?"

Nod.

"You prefer Eddie to Edwina?"

Nod.

She looked at me. There was something in that look, and I felt that something, and I put my hand down. There was silence in the second-grade room.

"Well, Eddie, thank you for that information."

I looked at the table. **SALLY HOBART** was silent. But when Mrs. Lattimore turned back to the board, Sally reached out to **EDWINA BECKEY** and carefully ripped off the **WINA** so it just read **ED BECKEY.**

Sally leaned toward me, her braids brushing the table, and whispered, "Hi, Eddie."

Every day, Willie does Sally's hair. The middle drawer of Sally's desk at her house is her hair drawer. Here is a list of Sally's hair ornaments:

1. Ponytail holders, large and small — glittered, neon, multicolored, lacy, beaded, sequined.
2. Barrettes of all shapes and sizes.
3. Tortoiseshell combs — to clip her hair back in their tortoiseshell teeth.
4. Chopsticks — to be thrust through a bun.
5. Hair bands.

6. Bandanas.
7. Tiny butterfly clips — which Willie arranges all over Sally's head when her hair is loose.

"But who'll do her hair?"

That's what I asked my mother that night we were standing in the kitchen with the buzzy fluorescent light above us and the little glass jar of eight-penny nails behind her.

"Sally can probably do her hair herself by now, don't you think?"

I stared at her. Had she never in all these years noticed Sally's hair? Had she not seen the way one day it would be French-braided in a coronet around her head, and the next, in a ponytail that began at the top of her head with just a few strands of hair and then went all the way down the back of her head — gathering in hair as it went, secured with six ponytail holders of different, complementary colors — and the next, in a two-strand weave? Had she not seen the way the butterfly clips twinkled in the sun when Sally was practicing her jump roping?

"No," I said. "No, Mom, she can't do her hair by herself."

 *Nine*

This past year we studied pack rats in earth science. Mr. Tyler created a midden heap for us in an unused desk well.

Mr. Tyler shone his pocket flashlight into the darkness of the unused well, revealing a little pile of things he had assembled: an acorn cap, some peanuts, half a broken comb, a silver thimble, a pinecone, and a clump of hair that looked as if he'd pulled it out of his wife's or daughter's hairbrush, because it was long and brown, not short and gray like his.

"Sixth graders, this is a representation of a pack rat's midden heap," Mr. Tyler said. That was what he always referred to us as: sixth graders.

The thin beam of light from his pocket flashlight glinted off the silver thimble.

"Are pack rats generally known for their sewing ability?" Tracy Benova asked.

"Pack rats like shiny objects," Mr. Tyler said.

He was used to Tracy's questions. Mr. Tyler played his flashlight beam around the rest of the dark desk well. Ancient chewing gum was stuck to the underside of the desktop.

"Sixth graders, imagine that you are pack rats," Mr. Tyler said. "What would you include in your personal midden heaps? Go back to your desks and think of objects that are precious to you. Make a list of them. Your list will be your two-dimensional midden heap."

I went back to my desk and lifted up the desktop to its highest degree of openness and rooted around with my hand in an attempt to find my notebook. Loose-leaf paper floated to the floor around me. I rummaged around and stuck myself with a pushpin, the same pushpin I had lost weeks ago. Weeks ago, at the moment I realized that the pushpin had been lost in the darkness of the well, I had made a mental note: *This pushpin will come back to haunt you.* And there it was. I pulled my hand out and sucked the blood off the tip of my ring finger, where the pushpin had pushed in.

This was my list:

1. The **bottle cap** that I keep rolled up in a sock in my top bureau drawer. It's the cap to the first bottle of Orangina I ever drank, and my father bought it for me when we were in Syracuse at the Carousel Mall. He put me on the carousel. I rode around and around, and every time I rode around, there was my father, waving. Then he bought me the Orangina, which I had never drunk before but had always wanted to.

2. A **letter** that my mother's sister Eva sent her from summer camp. She's my mother's

older sister, and I found the letter in a shoebox in the back of my parents' closet.

> *Dear Mildred,*
>
> *You will love camp when you come next year! My counselor is the best, and I am going to keep my fingers crossed that you get her too! We sleep in bunks and I am on the top. You can buy one candy bar a day from the canteen. You will love it here! Don't be scared, because I will be coming back next year too, so you will have a sister in case you get scared.*
>
> *XXXXXOOOOO, Eva*

"Mom?" I said after I found that letter and took it to my room. "Do you get scared?"

"Sure," she said. "Sometimes."

"Of what?"

"Well, I'm not a big fan of lightning, to be honest. Now that you're old enough to understand lightning on its own terms, I can tell you that. When you were little and scared of it, I used to pretend how much I loved lightning and thunder."

I wanted to tell my mother that I too get scared, terribly scared, and how much I want to be brave, but I didn't.

3. An **empty box**, tiny, with a hinged lid. It's made out of wood. I found it behind the Twin Churches when Sally and I were cutting through the woods on our way to Nine Mile Trailer Park.

4. The ***Rome Observer-Dispatch*** from the day I was born.

I remember watching Sally work on her list too. She doesn't like lists, but since it was an assignment, she had to make one. Her desk well was no doubt messless. Sally has little tolerance for disorder.

I tried to imagine what Sally might be putting on her list.

1. **Something to do with hair.** Maybe the first barrette her grandmother had ever given her?

2. Her **first jump rope,** the one she used to lead her imaginary dog, Roscoe, around with.

3. The **dictionary** that she won in the fourth grade at the state spelling bee in Syracuse.

4. Her **meander stick.**

5. The **miniature chair** that she got from one of the lumberjacks at the lumberjack show in Old Forge. Willie took us up to that show one summer. We were seven, the age of reason, the age we met. First we ate pancakes at Key's Pancake House, then we went to the lumberjack show.

6. A **chocolate-covered sprinkle dough-nut** from a long-ago Sunday, uneaten and preserved for posterity?

But I didn't know what Sally was really putting on her list. I couldn't even be sure that the objects I had put on my mental midden heap were the objects I truly wanted there.

If pack rats were people, they would be list people, like me.

Ten

"Mom?"

"Edwina?"

My mother often answers me that way. Instead of "Yes?" or "What?" she'll say my name.

"Would you say that most people are equipped for this world?"

My mother was folding towels on the living-room couch. All our towels are yellow, because yellow is my mother's favorite color.

"Are most people equipped for this world?" my mother repeated thoughtfully.

She finished folding a towel. She shakes each one out with a snap before she folds it. She laid the folded towel on top of the pile and smoothed the stack with her palm. The sun streamed in through the living-room window, and the pile of towels suddenly looked very beautiful to me.

"I think that most people figure out ways to cope with the world," my mother said. "Maybe that's a better way to put it."

She folded another towel. I watched her hands hover over the towel stack, and I knew she was debating whether or not to put the new towel on top of the stack or start a new stack. She started a new one, right next to the old one.

"We come into the world with no real defenses," my mother said. "We're pretty much helpless, as infants."

I pictured a newborn baby like the kind I sometimes saw in BJ's or in the diner. Mostly they slept. Occasionally they screamed, with their tiny faces squinched up and bright red.

"In the beginning, you have your parents to take care of you," my mother said. "And that works for a while. But after a while, you're more or less on your own. And if you haven't figured out ways to defend yourself, the world is a difficult place to live in."

The second towel stack was approaching the same height as the first. My mother likes to save up all the dirty towels so she can wash them all at once, one giant yellow load.

"I'm not talking just about ways to defend yourself against people who might say mean things to you, want to hurt you in some way," my mother said. "I'm talking about the world itself, the sadness in it, the way it can be so unfair."

I could tell she was choosing her words carefully. She had vowed never to lie to me.

"Sometimes I think that Jill never figured out how to protect herself from that kind of sadness," my mother said.

My mother finished folding the last towel. I looked out the living-room window at the sun, spreading fingers of light across the Sterns Valley. When I was little, I used to think light like that, in rays that play across the valley, looked like the legs of an unknown giant being, walking across the foothills and the valley and the meander and the trees next to our house. I used to think those rays were a glimpse into heaven. I used to ask my mother where heaven was.

"Where do *you* think heaven is, Edwina?" she always said.

Then I started asking *what* heaven was.

"What do *you* think heaven is, Edwina?"

My mother answers questions with questions.

Eleven

A few days later my mother and I drove up to
BJ's Foods in Remsen, the same as we do every
week. When the milk runs out, it's grocery day.

My mother takes the big cart and starts in
the soup and noodles aisle.

I get one of the green baskets and go straight
to produce. My job is to pick out whatever vegetables and fruit I think we might like, enough
to last us until the milk runs out.

Among the fruits and vegetables is where
I like to be. All the beautiful colors: purple

eggplant, orange carrots, green broccoli, red apples. When we made our color wheels in first grade, I made mine in the colors of vegetables.

That day, an old man was in BJ's, picking out apples. His hands shook the way some old people's hands shake. He could hardly hold a single apple. There was a pyramid of them, and the old man tried to pick one up from the bottom row, and the whole pyramid fell. Apples tumbled every which way. The old man kept turning his head to look at the apples rolling all over the swept floor of the vegetable section. A feeling flickered through me, the same shadow feeling that I had felt that day on the school bus when I had willed Willie to appear and she had not appeared.

I ran after the apples and picked them all up. I wished I could pick them all up and pile them back into their pyramid, undo what had happened, so that the old man would not have to stand there like that with that look on his face.

When I was done, and the apples were heaped back onto their apple shelf not in a pyramid, just in a heap, I looked up and Jill was standing next to me, looking at the old man. He had that look on his face. His hands were still trembling.

"Jill," I said. I couldn't say what I wanted to say, which is how awful it was seeing the old man like that, an empty plastic bag in one trembling hand.

She knelt down next to me and put her arm around me.

"It's hard, isn't it, Eddie?" she said. She tucked my hair behind my ear. "It's so hard, sometimes."

I had never heard Jill's voice before.

The next time I was at Sally and Willie's house, I felt as if I were carrying a secret inside me.

I wanted to tell Sally about the old man and the tumbling apples. I wanted to tell Sally about her mother's voice that day in the produce section, how quiet it was, how gentle.

What I really wanted to talk about was Jill, how she had been fifteen when she had Sally, how when you think about it, she had been only three or four years older than we are now. I wanted to talk about sadness, and unfairness, and defenses.

But I didn't know how.

"Sally, do you remember the first day we met?" is what I heard myself saying.

We were sitting in her living room, not doing anything. Sally didn't want to play Monopoly. She didn't want to jump rope. She didn't want to go see how the blue bicycle was doing. She didn't even want to do earth science experiments in the kitchen.

Willie was upstairs, taking a nap. I had never known Willie to take a nap before.

"The day we met?" Sally said. "What day was that?"

"The first day of second grade, of course."

"No," Sally said. "I have no idea what you're talking about."

Then she said it again.

"I have no idea what you're talking about."

"Sally. The first day of second grade, back by the hedgehog cage."

She gave me a look.

"You and I didn't meet in second grade," she said.

"What are you talking about?" I said. "We met on the very first day of second grade, when Mrs. Lattimore sat us together at that table back by the hedgehog cage."

"No, we didn't."

She kept looking at me.

I didn't know what to say.

We sat there, silent in her living room, while the sky turned orange and pink over the foothills to the west. William T. Jones's house on Jones Hill glowed white for a second as the sun dropped. I looked at Sally and she looked right back at me.

I wanted to talk about the first day of second grade, and the dress Willie had worn, bright green with yellow polka dots, swinging around her like a tent. All of us second graders watched Willie standing and laughing with the teacher, Sally-the-new-girl holding her hand and wearing a dark jumper and standing slightly behind her grandmother, so that a fold of bright green cloth half-covered her. The brightest thing about Sally was her hair, her beautiful hair, falling in two smooth braids on either side of her face. I wanted to talk about the bicycle tree.

What I wanted to talk about was Willie, about the disease in her blood.

I snapped my purple rubber band and tried again.

"There was a hedgehog cage, and there was a hedgehog in it, and the hedgehog's name was Hedgy. Sally! Come on! You're the one who *named* it."

"I would never give any animal such a stupid name."

There was a look in her eyes.

"That would be like calling a cat Catty or a sheep Sheepy," Sally said. "I would've chosen a much better name for the second-grade hedgehog, had there ever even been a hedgehog in second grade."

"Okay," I said carefully. "You don't remember Hedgy, and you don't remember the table with the name tapes on it. Do you remember being in Mrs. Lattimore's class at all, then?"

"I wasn't in Mrs. Lattimore's class for second grade; I was in Mr. Marconi's."

She smiled.

"Mr. Marconi was really nice. Every Friday he gave us the choice of a popcorn party or extra recess."

I stared at her.

"We all loved Mr. Marconi."

I thought, *Is this what happens when a person loses her mind? Is this what a nervous breakdown is?*

Because there is no Mr. Marconi. There

never has been a Mr. Marconi. Sterns Elementary is a tiny school in a tiny town in the foothills of the Adirondack Mountains, and there is only one second-grade teacher. And that second-grade teacher is Mrs. Lattimore, and like it or not, every single second grader in Sterns Elementary is taught by Mrs. Lattimore.

"How can you not remember Mr. Marconi?" Sally said. "His classroom was right across the hall from Mrs. Lattimore's."

Her eyes were looking away from me, out the kitchen window that looked onto the foothills in the distance. She smiled, as if she was remembering a happy day in Mr. Marconi's class, a day with a popcorn party or extra recess, a day that never happened.

Twelve

"Why would someone not talk?"

"Why would *someone* not talk?" my mother said. "Are you talking about a hypothetical some-one, or are you talking about Jill Hobart?"

It was no use trying to hide something from my mother.

"I'm talking about Jill Hobart," I said.

"I don't know," my mother said.

"Does she have a complete tongue?"

My mother looked at me.

"What do you mean, 'Does she have a complete tongue?'"

I shrugged.

"I read in the medical encyclopedia that if you're missing part of your tongue, it's hard to talk, is all," I said.

"I imagine it would be."

"For example, it could have been chopped off in an accident," I said. "Jill could have been sitting in the front seat of a car that came to a very abrupt halt right while she was in the middle of taking a bite of a sandwich, and her teeth could have gone right through her tongue and chopped off the end of it."

"Have you been spending a lot of time thinking about this?" my mother said.

I shrugged again.

"Have you made a list?"

I shook my head.

I had, though. I had made a list of possible reasons why Jill Hobart didn't talk. Then I had ripped it up. After I made the list I had felt as if

I were spying on Sally and her grandmother and her mother. As if I were disturbing something that had been put in place long ago, a routine that didn't involve me, a routine in which Jill was the cashier for lane number 3 at BJ's Foods, and Willie walked the roads with her green pail, and Sally grew up happy in her house with her grandmother.

I can still remember the list, though.

Possible reasons why Jill doesn't talk
1. Incomplete tongue.
2. Extremely shy.
3. Nothing to say.
4. Speech impediment.
5. Doesn't speak English.
6. Cat's got her tongue.
7. Unknown.

I put number 6 on there to make myself laugh, but I didn't laugh, so I crossed it off. I studied the others. Shy — that was a possibility. But Jill wasn't so shy that she was a hermit. She worked every day at BJ's, and many people liked her. I personally knew of people who, even if another checkout line was shorter, would wait in Jill's line because she was a nice person. That's what everyone always said about Jill, that she was a nice person. I crossed off number 2.

My mother had said that Jill's tongue was fine, so I crossed off number 1.

Having a speech impediment would have been my best guess, had I not heard Jill's voice that day in the produce section of BJ's. Her voice had been soft and clear.

I crossed off number 4.

Number 3: nothing to say? I crossed that one off for its sheer impossibility.

Number 5 was just dumb, so I crossed that one off too.

That left only number 7: unknown.

Thirteen

The way Sundays used to be, Willie and Sally and I would sit around the table, eating chocolate-covered sprinkle doughnuts. That used to be our routine. It was our routine as long as I can remember. But I hadn't been to Sally's house on a Sunday morning all summer.

"Edwina, why don't you ride your bike over to Sally's house?" my mother said.

I looked at her. She looked back at me. It was a Sunday morning. Did she know what I was thinking? Did she know that I was scared,

scared to go to Sally's house, scared that everything would have changed, scared that those Sunday mornings, the way they used to be, would never happen again?

"Go on," she said. "Your friend needs you."

I rode my bike over to Sally's. I hadn't eaten breakfast. I was used to not eating breakfast on Sunday mornings so as to save room for doughnuts with Sally and Willie. Even though I was hungry, it didn't seem right to eat breakfast at my own house.

There were no doughnuts at Sally's house. No doughnut plate — the green china plate with the watermelon slices painted onto it that Willie got for a wedding present — sat in the middle of the table. No pyramid of doughnuts, the special doughnut pyramid that Willie always made. There was just Sally, sitting at the table. "Your friend needs you," my mother had said.

The shadowy feeling came crawling through me again.

"Hi," I said.

Nothing.

"Where's Willie?" I tried again.

Sally pointed upstairs. She didn't look at me.

"Sleeping?" I tried.

Nod.

"Did you already eat breakfast?" I said.

Sally shook her head.

What is the right thing to do when your friend needs you but she won't talk and you don't know what to say? I sat down in my chair at the table. Sally said nothing. I thought of Willie upstairs, sleeping, and I wondered if she was really awake and listening for sounds of conversation between Sally and me, conversation that wasn't happening. I started to lean back in my chair and then caught myself.

Snap, went the yellow rubber band.

And then the door opened and Jill was there. She stood in the doorway. In that moment, looking at her as she stood in the doorway, I saw how shy Jill was. When you're a kid you don't often think of grown-ups as shy. Jill pointed to the door and inclined her head, and I understood that Sally and I were to go with her. Where to? I didn't ask.

We crammed into Jill's car, Jill at the wheel, Sally next to her, me next to Sally. We made our way up to Queen of the Frosties. It was a late-summer day, and the sky was absolutely blue, and the foothills were the dark green they are just before the orange and the red and the gold.

I had never been to Queen of the Frosties with Sally or Jill. Sometimes, when he's not on the road, my father takes me up there on Saturday morning and we sit in a booth together, me next to my father, and his friends sitting across from us. I had never sat at the counter before.

But I did on this day, on a twirlable stool next to Sally. First I started twirling, and then she did. When two people sit next to each other on stools that twirl, each pushing off, pushing off, pushing off, the danger of catching knees and elbows midtwirl is great. It adds to the excitement.

Bang!

That would be me and Sally colliding. You twirl and twirl and twirl, the diner flashing by, a merry-go-round gone nuts. Your brain scrambles. The world spins itself into a not-world. There's a flash of red, a flash of chrome, a flash of dooropening-doorshutting-plateofeggsonthe-counter-Sophiethemorningwaitresspouringcoffee-rowofphotosclippedabovethegrilland *bang!*

You're on your behind on the linoleum.

Sally started to laugh the way she laughs, her head going up and down, her long braids trembling against her back. I had not seen her laugh in so long.

Jill and Sophie, the morning waitress, looked down at us on the floor. Dinerworld spun around me, because my brain hadn't caught up to the fact that I was no longer twirling.

Sally and I hauled ourselves back up onto

our stools. Our breakfasts were there in front of us.

Me: the 222 special.

1. Two scrambled eggs.
2. Two pancakes.
3. Two pieces of bacon.

Price: $2.22.

Sally: the farmer's breakfast.

1. A cast-iron pan with hash browns at the bottom.
2. Corned beef hash on top of the hash browns.
3. Two fried eggs on top of the corned beef hash.
4. Cheese melted on top of everything.

Price: $3.60.

A man two seats down from Jill: blueberry pancakes. If you order blueberry pancakes at Queen of the Frosties, you get a plate with three giant blue circles on it. They mix the blueberries into the pancake batter at the outset, rather than ladling a spoonful onto the pancakes when the pancakes are on the grill, so everything turns blue. The yellow lump on top is butter, scooped with an ice-cream scoop out of a big butter pail. That's how they do it at Queen of the Frosties. Price: $3.10.

Jill: coffee. Black coffee. Price: on the house, because Sophie is her friend.

That's exactly what Sophie said: "On the house, Miss Jill, because you are my friend." Sophie has the same color hair as Sally, but Sophie's hair is straight. Not a curl or even the hint of a wave in Sophie's hair. And there's a teeny bit of gray even though Sophie is young, younger even than Jill. Sophie doesn't seem to care that Jill doesn't talk.

When we were halfway through our breakfast and Jill was on her second cup of coffee, Sophie handed Sally and me a paper bag.

"Here," she said. "My treat. Maybe you can use them down at your hut when you go camping."

Sophie knows how much I love the hen-and-rooster salt and pepper shakers at Queen of the Frosties, the salt hen, the pepper rooster. You could say I covet them. When I go to the Queen with my father, Sophie sometimes gives me the job of refilling the salt shakers while he talks with his friends. You always put in a few grains of rice when you refill a salt shaker. That's so the salt doesn't clump together.

In the bag was a new pair, with the price tag still on them. Queen of the Frosties salt and pepper shakers are popular. The Queen is right on Route 12, so it gets a lot of trucker traffic, a lot of tourists heading up north into the Adirondacks. The shakers were disappearing, so the Queen ordered a ton and started selling them. "Buy Yourself a Bit of Adirondack Folklore," the sign says.

"Thank you, Sophie," I said. That was all I said. Sophie isn't the kind of person you gush around. *"Sophie is a girl not given to melodrama,"* I remembered Willie saying once about her.

Sally was eating her way through layer after layer of her farmer's breakfast. She didn't excavate all the layers in a single forkful. She ate her way down: first the cheese, then the eggs, then the corned beef hash, then the hash browns.

"You always get Sunday off?"

That was Sophie talking to Jill while we sat on our stools and ate our breakfasts. Jill nodded.

"Me, I'm thinking of asking for every Sunday off. Think of it, every Saturday night and the whole day Sunday too."

Jill nodded again.

"How's your mom?" Sophie said.

Jill looked away, down the counter. Sophie studied her.

I watched them, the grown-ups, semi-grown-ups because they seemed so young — Jill in a Mickey Mouse sweatshirt, Sophie in her Queen of the Frosties T-shirt and her jeans and her white sneakers — Sophie talking in her quiet voice to Jill, Jill nodding or shaking her head, while I ate my way down to the china on my plate and Sally's fork started scraping against the cast iron of her skillet. I pictured Willie in her bed at Sally's house. Did she know it was a Sunday morning, and did she wish she could get up and walk down Route 274 to Jewell's and come back with a white waxed paper bag filled with sprinkle doughnuts?

Fourteen

"Willie has good days, and she has bad days," my mother said when I asked.

On the good days, Willie walked down to Fraser Road and back with her pail. Willie's a cattail picker. She especially likes the ones that grow in the swamp on either side of 274 just before it intersects with Fraser Road. To me, cattails have always looked like brown velvet hot dogs.

Jill dropped us off at Sally's house after the diner. Willie was sitting at the kitchen table. She smiled when we came in. Sally started toward her and then stopped. I knew, I could feel in my own skin, how much Sally wanted to sit on Willie's lap. But she didn't.

"How's the hovel these days, girls?" Willie said. "Still holding?"

Sally said nothing.

"Still holding," I said.

"Then, isn't it about time you girls went camping?" Willie said.

I looked down at the table. The red-and-white-checked tablecloth was on. Willie must have spread it when she got up. Sally said nothing. I traced one of the red checks.

"I decree that you, Sally Wilmarth Hobart, and you, Edwina Stiles Beckey, shall go camping at the Cabin next weekend," Willie said.

We were silent. Willie looked from Sally to me and back. She looked tired. You could see it in her eyes, and in the lines around her mouth, which I had never noticed before.

"Do you want me to do your hair, Sally?" Willie said.

Sally shook her head. Her hair was loose, floating around her head like a nimbus, which is a word we had learned that year in earth science.

Willie had decreed that we would go camping, so we went camping.

When we got to the Cabin, Sally and I took all our food out of our grocery bags. We use doubled-up grocery bags instead of backpacks, forgetting every time that a mile through a cornfield, through woods, and down a hill while lugging a doubled-up grocery bag in front of you is not all that easy.

This is what we had before us:

1. Hot dogs.
2. White bread.
3. Cinnamon-apple instant oatmeal.
4. Breath mints.
5. Salami.
6. Jar of cracked green olives.

7. Loaf of French bread.
8. Plastic container of blueberries.
9. Can of pineapple rings.
10. Can of baked beans.

Here is some of what we forgot, which was a lot:

1. A pot.
2. A can opener.
3. Graham crackers and marshmallows and chocolate bars.
4. Matches.

Here is what we couldn't eat because of what we forgot:

1. Instant oatmeal.
2. Pineapple rings.
3. Baked beans.

Here is what we did eat:

1. A cold hot dog each, Sally's wrapped in white bread, mine solo.

2. Four slices of hard salami hacked off with my pocketknife.
3. Some French bread broken off the loaf the way Willie told us they break it off in France.
4. Twelve green olives.

Sally then ate one half of another cold hot dog, wrapped around with another slice of white bread, and five breath mints.

It wasn't the dinner we had pictured. Most aren't, at the Cabin.

That's because of the no-list rule.

I went inside the Cabin after our un-dinner, which because of the falling-downness of the Cabin and its lack of windowpanes is in a way like being still outside. I sat at the table, which Sally's grandmother — *Willie* — had bought for us at a garage sale in Remsen.

"Consider this a hovel-warming gift," Willie

said the day she dragged it down to the Cabin, tied onto Sally's old red wagon. Willie had to take off two of the legs to get it through the tiny door, which meant another trip back up the hill and through the cornfield to get a screwdriver.

I watched from the paneless window as Sally picked up her meander stick and walked over to her measuring spot. She stood next to the meander, the stream that flows into Nine Mile Creek, and lowered her stick into the water. She picked that stick up one day a few summers ago. She scraped all the bark off it so that it was smooth and shiny. Then she created a measuring system on the stick, lines and dots and slashes, incomprehensible. Every time she's at the Cabin, she goes to that one spot and puts her meander stick in the water to measure its depth.

She didn't say anything to me, even when I went over and sat beside her, watching her writing down her incomprehensible notes.

It was late August, the cornstalks in the field as high as our heads. On hot days Sally and

I used to play hide-and-seek in the cornfield. I used to count to one hundred and then stay still and listen for the sound of leaves brushing against Sally as she snuck around the rows.

Have you ever walked through a cornfield when the corn is higher than your head? The sun filters through the green. The roots of the stalks grip the ground like claws. In a summer of enough rain and enough sun, you wouldn't believe how tall the corn can get by the end of August, so much taller than you, so much higher than you ever expected it to be.

Fifteen

I dragged first one folding chair and then the other out of the Cabin and set them up next to the meander, where Sally was crouched with her meander stick.

They were bright red, our folding chairs. Willie had gotten them for us at a garage sale in Sterns: two dollars each. A little green price sticker was still affixed to the back of each.

"Sit," I said.

Sally sat. I sat next to her. I closed my eyes so as to see if I could sense the sun on my face growing cooler as the sun went down. I wanted to use only my sense of the air, warmed by the sun. It was the next-best thing to playing Blind. I tipped back to catch the long slanting rays of the sun on my face.

"Don't do that," Sally said.

"Do what?" I said. My eyes were closed. It was hard to tell if the air was growing cooler or not. I realized how much I used my eyes to determine how something felt. I wonder how it is for people who are truly blind. Their sense of touch must be so much better than mine, not having sight to help it along.

"Don't tip back in your chair."

"Oh," I said. "Sorry."

I tipped my chair back upright and squinched my eyes shut so as to block out all sense of light. But then colors started swirling behind my closed eyelids. You know how that happens.

Snap!

A sharp pain stung my wrist.

My eyes flew open. "What!" I said. "What did you do that for?"

A bright red line flushed up across my skin from where Sally had snapped my yellow rubber band.

"Because you were tipping back in your chair again," she said.

"So what? I've been tipping back in chairs my whole life," I said. "And so have you."

"Not anymore."

"Since when?"

She didn't answer me. She just sat back in her red folding chair and folded her arms and scowled at the setting sun. I suddenly wished that she had a rubber band on her own wrist, one that I could snap. Hard.

"What is wrong with you?" I said.

"What's wrong with *you,* you mean."

"Tip, tip, tip," I said. "Big deal."

"You can get hurt that way."

"No, you can't."

I tipped back as far as I could, so far that I

felt a moment of fright when it seemed as if I was about to go splat on my back. But I kept a poker face, just in case Sally was watching, and I stared up at the sky. The moon was already out, and pretty soon stars would start to reveal themselves.

Boom!

I was slammed back down to earth, all four folding-chair legs firm on the ground. Sally stood over me. I stared back at her.

"You can *die* that way!" she shouted. "Grandma's friend Sara *died* that way!"

 *Sixteen*

I woke in the night. Sound, familiar, was all about me: crickets, a whippoorwill whooping in its endless way, the breeze in the tops of the white pines. It took me a minute to realize that I was in a sleeping bag, camping out at the Cabin.

The sound that woke me was not familiar, although it was a cornstalk sound. It didn't have the rustle of raccoons prowling around, shaking the stalks for ripe ears. It was the sound of someone moving through the cornfield, someone who was familiar with this particular darkness, who knew where the Cabin was.

I reached to shake Sally's sleeping bag but she was asleep, deep asleep, and I remembered how she had snapped my yellow rubber band against my wrist, so hard, and how we had gone to bed without saying anything to each other, without counting the calls of the whippoorwills out loud, our routine, and I did not want to wake her.

The rustling grew closer.

I felt for my purple rubber band.

Snap.

Fight or flight, we learned one day in earth science. It's the natural response to fear. You either run and hide, or you stay and fight with everything you have in you. You are focused only on survival. Nothing else matters. I can still see Mr. Tyler and the way he stroked chalk onto the chalkboard with big sweeping moves of his arm. He prefers yellow to white. He used to take a box of white chalk into Mrs. Fencher's next-door room, knowing that he was a lone yellow-chalk man among users of white, and return triumphant with a box of yellow.

Mr. Tyler is a tall man with gray hair and a big belly that he slings his belt under instead of into. I can imagine Mr. Tyler fighting, but I can't imagine him fleeing.

He told us that if you're scared enough, you will pee your pants. I was more scared than I had ever been, listening to that rustling coming toward me, and one part of my mind was waiting to feel my sleeping bag turn warm and wet, but it didn't happen.

Rustle.

I wanted to wake Sally. I wanted her to listen to the sound and tell me what it was. I wanted to hear that tone in her voice, the tone that means: *The answer has come to me.* I've seen answers come over Sally. Occasionally in class, when the teacher asks a very difficult question — one that he asks with the tone of voice that lets us know he doesn't expect anyone to know the answer and has in fact asked the question just to let us off the hook, a sort of introduction to that particular topic — Sally will sit up a certain way. Her hand will raise itself into the air. All fingers will be extended and rigid. The look will be on her face. Her lips will be parted. The class will turn to look at her as maybe all those people standing on the coast of the Red Sea might have looked at Moses as he parted the waters and passed right on through.

"Yes? Sally?"

And the answers come spilling forth.

The power of one thousand.

Franklin Delano Roosevelt.

Zeno's paradox.

Sojourner Truth.

Macbeth, *by William Shakespeare.*

That's the kind of answer that Sally comes out with. You wouldn't expect it, because usually Sally is thought of as smart but not extra smart. A pretty ordinary student. An ordinary girl who, even though Willie can do her hair any kind of way she might ever want, likes her hair best in braids, ordinary braids.

Rustle.

I forgot about how hard Sally had snapped my yellow rubber band.

I wanted to wake Sally and have her tell me what the sound was, but in the moonlight her face looked so peaceful, and I realized that it had been some time since I had seen her look that peaceful, and again I could not wake her.

I turned my head, searching the sky for signs of the mountains rising up. Where were they? They needed to be there, my foothills, rising up out of a pink and orange sunrise. *Please be there.* I squinted my eyes, and twisted my head so that I was looking straight up at the sky. A pale fingernail of moon hovered in the far west, and stars glimmered faintly above me. When next I looked to the east, the sunrise was there, but in its very beginnings, more of a lightening of the darkness than anything you would call light.

And there was Jill, sitting next to Sally on the damp ground.

I knew her by the outline of her shoulders and neck, bent as they were over Sally. Sally was asleep, and I lay as still as I could, hardly breathing, watching Jill watch Sally sleep. Jill's hand came up, two fingers, and she stroked the wisps of hair back from Sally's forehead.

All was still, and in the moonlight everything was shades of gray. Flickers of light caught my eye, like fireflies twirling — little fairies is how Sally and I used to think of them — dancing around in the air. The flickers were the meander, water flowing slowly in its bends and curves, moonlight reflected off it.

Jill saw that I was awake. Her two fingers did not stop moving on Sally's head, smoothing and stroking the hair back. Back, and back, and back, Jill stroked the wisps of hair. Behind her the meander sparkled, as if it were something alive, something signaling to me in its own kind of water Morse code.

She looked at me. I couldn't see what her eyes were saying in the darkness.

"Jill?" I whispered.

She tilted her head in a way that meant *Yes?*

There was so much to say, and there was nothing to say. Willie was going to die, sooner rather than later, and what would happen to Sally? Then a feeling came churning up from inside me, from farther down than I could have thought a feeling could come from, and it swept through me. I had felt glimpses of this feeling, shadows of it, when I had stood next to Jill at BJ's and watched the old man's hands, and the apples tumbling and rolling in all directions. I had felt more shadows of it all summer, when I had ridden my bike down 274 and there was no Willie tromping along with her green pail. Once, I had felt the shadow of this feeling when

I was walking up the driveway to Sally's house and had seen the outline of Willie pass behind the living-room window.

The name of the feeling was grief.

It came swarming up inside me and choked me. I saw my hand reaching to Jill. She left Sally and came over to me.

"Jill," I whispered.

What could I say? How could I tell her what I was feeling, when the feeling was huge, choking me up inside? I looked up at her, silent Jill, whose eyes were shadowed in the darkness. Jill, who had stood beside me at BJ's as the apples tumbled and rolled.

I watched as tears gathered themselves in Jill's eyes and spilled down her cheeks, tiny bright trails in the moonlight. It came to me then that Jill was losing her mother.

"I know," she said. Her voice was a whisper, like mine. She picked my hand up and held it between both of hers. Her fingers were warm.

She put her head close to mine. Sally slept on.

Slender fingers of orange and pink began to glimmer in the eastern sky, and Jill got up. I propped myself up on one elbow and watched as she made her soundless way back to the cornfield, until the cornstalks had swallowed her up and the rustling sound of her passage grew too faint to hear.

Seventeen

I want to be not afraid.

But in reality I'm scared by many things.

The night sky scares me. I hate being scared of the night sky, because the night sky is beautiful, is a thing of beauty on a summer night in the Adirondacks when the stars are flung across the darkness like diamonds on black velvet.

My mother once woke me in the middle of the night when I was about four years old, long before the age of reason. She carried me downstairs and stood me up on the porch with her.

She held my hand. Above us the sky pulsed with color: green and blue and red and yellow.

"It's the aurora borealis," my mother said.

I was so tired I could barely keep my eyes open, there on the porch, holding her hand, looking up at that unearthly sight, but I was not yet scared. It was only later that fear set in, fear of its mystery, its endlessness. The way it goes on forever, an infinity of miles past where breath can be taken, past where there is gravity and atmosphere and the sun that I so love watching come up, day after day after familiar day.

Fear came to me one night when we were camping down at the Cabin. I lay in my sleeping bag, looking up at the unlightness of the sky. Sally and I were pointing out constellations to each other: Orion, the Big Dipper, the Little Dipper. She knew Cassiopeia too. But every other star in that dark sky was unknown to me, and to Sally, and probably to most of the people in the world. After a while Sally and I stopped talking, and I could tell by the sound of her breath — deep and long and slow — that she was asleep.

A shooting star streaked across the blackness, and I shivered. It came to me that there was mystery not only beyond my own solar system but in my tiny ordinary life, down here on earth, where I lay stretched out on my back in my flannel-lined sleeping bag.

Why was I in this world?

The stars so far above me glittered on in their mute way and brought me no answers. Fear came to me in the feeling that for the rest of my life I would be asking this question, and that the answer might forever be unknowable.

Eighteen

We had never before had guests at the Cabin. They must have parked on the road up by William T. Jones's house, held the barbed wire for each other, and made their way down the pasture toward where they knew the Cabin was even though they couldn't see it behind the white pines, the white pines with their arching lofted branches.

It was early morning.

I didn't see them until they were already close to the Cabin, making their way along the meander. Willie had her green pail in her hand and

Jill held her arm. Their progress was slow. You could say they were ambling. Meandering, even.

The sunlight struck sparks off the water.

"Look," I said, pointing them out to Sally.

Her face changed. She picked up her jump rope and moved off to the side of the Cabin. She started jumping, her back to me. She started with some cancans, then she started to practice her backward triple under. The backward triple under is the hardest trick. Only a few people at our school can do one.

"Sal?" I said. "Do you want to go out with me and meet them?"

The jump rope scurried around in the worn patch of dirt by the Cabin. I watched it twist and wiggle for a while, watched Sally's face get tighter and more frowning with each failed attempt.

I dragged one of the red folding chairs out of the Cabin and set it up outside, in a patch of sun, near where Sally was practicing her backward triple under. Then I made sure that the planks over the meander were set tight into each mud wall. As they came closer, I saw that Willie was leaning on Jill's arm. Her green pail didn't bounce up and down the way it usually did, the way it used to, back when Willie tromped up and down Route 274 every day.

"Greetings!" I called. I scissored my arms the way Willie used to when she saw our school bus pass by. "Welcome, all ye who enter here!"

Willie looked down at the planks.

"Excellent construction," she said. "Aesthetically pleasing and useful at the same time. A triumph of form and function."

Sally was still practicing her backward triple under in the jump-rope dirt patch. She didn't look over at us. She didn't come running over to see what was in the pail, which were doughnuts in a white waxed paper bag from Jewell's.

I picked an overgrown rhubarb leaf to serve as a plate for the doughnuts. It was a precarious arrangement. One sudden tremble of a wrist and the whole thing would come tumbling down. I held it out to Willie.

"Doughnut?" I said.

She looked up at me from the red folding chair, the seat of honor, in an appraising way.

"Excuse me," I said. "What I mean to say is, Willie, would you like a doughnut?"

"No thank you, Eddie," she said.

I have tried to train myself into calling Willie Willie. I have snapped and snapped and snapped my blue rubber band. But it's not always easy. It needs to begin in the mind, retraining your brain to substitute a different word for the word you've used for so long.

"Sally," Willie called. "Treat for you!"

Sally came over. Still, she wouldn't look at her grandmother or Jill. I held out the rhubarb-leaf plate of doughnuts to her, but she shook her head.

"Are you sure?" I said.

She shook her head.

"If you have one, I'll have one," Willie said. Shake.

Then Willie, the anti-sugarist, did something I had never seen her do. She plucked one of the sprinkle doughnuts off the rhubarb leaf and took a bite. She closed her eyes and held her face up to the sun.

"*Mmm,*" she said. "Delectable."

Sally stood there, holding her jump rope. Willie held the bitten doughnut toward her.

"Bite? They're your favorite food."

"Used to be," Sally said.

She wiggled the jump rope so that it looked like a blue-and-green snake dancing in the dirt. Willie took another bite.

"Sugar's bad for you," Sally said. "That's what you've always told me."

"Sugar might be bad for you," Willie said. "I've always held that opinion, it's true. But lately it's come to me that if an opportunity for sweetness presents itself, who am I to refuse?"

Willie took another bite. I wondered how sugar on the tongue of an anti-sugarist, after so long without sugar, tasted. Was it good? I thought of all the Sunday mornings in the past when Sally and I had sat at the kitchen table with Willie and Willie had laughed and shaken her head when we teased her, trying to get her to take a bite of one of our sprinkle doughnuts. I watched her now, chewing and swallowing. Was she thinking about those Sunday mornings too? Did she regret them now, all the sugar she had missed out on?

Nineteen

Not long ago Sally and I were sitting in her kitchen, eating doughnuts. My mother had just told me about the disease that was harming Willie's blood. Willie and Jill were standing outside in the sunshine, next to the little red storage shed where they keep the lawn mower and the wheelbarrow. Jill's head was bent, and Willie's arms moved as she talked. Jill was the listener and Willie, the talker.

Jill's head was bent and Willie leaned toward her. I could tell from the careful way

Willie's hands moved, and the slow curve of her back, that her voice was quiet. Maybe she used to hold Jill on her lap when Jill was a little girl, the same way that Sally now sat on her lap. Maybe she had braided Jill's hair too, tied ribbons on the end the way they were tied in the one school picture of Jill that Sally had once shown me.

Willie's hands had moved in the sunlight, describing slow circles and shapes that I couldn't define. Was she telling Jill how to make spaghetti sauce with the secret V8 ingredient, the way Sally and I like it, the way we've had it a thousand times at their house? Was she telling Jill how to fold Sally's shirts when they come out of the dryer or, in the summer, off the line? Because Sally's fussy about shirts.

Was it possible that Willie had been showing Jill how to braid Sally's hair? Maybe Jill didn't know how to braid and Willie was trying to explain it to her, how you separate a river of hair into three tributaries and weave them together, over and under, over and under, until they have become a river again, but a different kind of river, not smooth and straight as once it was, but beautiful in a different kind of way.

Maybe Willie had been showing Jill how to do Sally's hair, for the time when she herself couldn't do it anymore.

The rhubarb leaf lay next to the meander, Willie's half-eaten doughnut resting upon it. I lay down beside it, on my back, and looked up at the morning sky. The moon hung high above me, barely noticeable, a slender curve of white. My nursery school teacher told us that a day-light moon is known as the children's moon.

I thought about Willie. I thought about how we all carry rivers within us, streams and mean-ders and tributaries of blood, how it's a mirac-ulous thing, bringing us life every minute of every day.

I reached out and stroked my finger along the edge of the rhubarb leaf, then licked it. Anyone watching me might have thought that I was a girl greedy for more doughnut, eager for the last crumb of colored sprinkle. But that's not what I was doing. Can you imagine it yourself, the taste of the first doughnut hole I ever ate, and how it felt on my tongue, on that late-summer day in the foothills of the Adirondack Mountains?

Twenty

Sally picked up her meander stick and dragged it over to the place where she takes her measurements. Her hair was tangled down her back, and the sight of it, messy and uncared-for, hurt me. I sat next to her and tried to follow the sight line of her hazel eyes, her eyes that wouldn't look at me.

"Sally, you know the blue bicycle?" I said. "It isn't a blue bicycle any longer. It's changed into something else. It's evolved."

She angled her head farther away from me.

"My whole life, I've walked by that tree and looked up to see the blue bicycle," I said. "And now I walk by and it's not a bike anymore, but it's not a tree either."

She didn't make any indication that she had heard me.

"It must have been changing all this time," I said. "All these years, it's been turning into something else."

I looked at her not looking at me, and I remembered the first time I saw her, with her braids, back at the hedgehog table. I felt for the purple rubber band on my wrist.

"Sally," I said.

I was almost crying. I remembered the way she used to bend her head over her workbook when we were practicing uppercase and lowercase, how she used to stroke Hedgy's fur with the tip of one finger, and how I used to look at her hair, her beautiful hair in its Willie braids.

She wouldn't look at me, wouldn't look at me, wouldn't.

"My mother remembers the first day of second grade," I said suddenly. "Way in the back by the hedgehog cage. She was there; she came to pick me up, and she remembers you being there."

Sally laughed.

"She's lying," she said.

"My mother never lies."

"She's got a lousy memory, then," she said. "Just like you."

My eyes hurt. Throbbed with the tears that wanted to come out, that I wouldn't let come out.

"Or maybe she needs glasses too."

Sally reached out and snapped my purple band.

Then she snapped them all.

Hard.

"You and your lists!" she said. "Like you

think you can actually control anything that's going to happen to you."

"Why are you doing this?" I said.

"Doing what?"

"Lying."

"Who's lying, Edwina?"

Edwina. Sally had never called me Edwina. From that very first day, Sally had always called me Eddie. Eddie's my name.

"You are," I said.

"No," she said. "I'm not lying."

Sally's head was tipped up into the air so that her chin stuck straight toward me. I could see that she was going to say *no* to every single question I asked her, and it was useless to ask her anything, anything about our entire lives together, but I couldn't stop. I kept on going.

"Is your hair long?"

"No."

"Is your T-shirt green?"

"No."

"Is your mother's name Jill?"

"No."

I stood there in the sunshine, watching the light play off the red strands in Sally's beautiful hair, her hair that I had always wanted for myself, and I watched as her chin never tilted downward and her eyes stared back at me with that look in them.

"Does your grandmother do your hair every day?"

"My grandmother never does my hair."

"Have I been your friend since second grade?"

She smiled.

"Do I even know you?" she said.

I saw the meander stick out of the corner of my eye and it reminded me of Willie, and the keep-away-the-dogs sticks she used to carry, and the way she used to swing down the road as if it were her own road.

"Sally Hobart, is your grandmother sick?"

Sally stood there in the sun, with her chin in the air. I will see her that way forever. Behind her the Adirondacks rose up, blue gray in the afternoon sunshine.

"Is your grandmother never going to get better?"

There she stood, with her hair quivering about her neck as if it were alive.

My voice was quiet, and it was slow. It was nearly a whisper.

"Is your grandmother dying?"

"No," Sally said.

But it wasn't Sally's voice. It wasn't the voice that I thought of as Sally's, her voice with its hoarse sound that I was so used to. It is possible to love someone very much and know that if you say a certain thing in a certain way, it will hurt her terribly, and yet you say it anyway.

Twenty-one

Sally stayed next to the meander the rest of that day, that long day, without words. Late in the afternoon I went inside the Cabin and stayed there for quite a while, holding the salt and pepper shakers, one in each hand. Out the paneless window to the west, the last of the sun was stroking the shoulders of the foothills. The curtains we made so long ago out of one of Sally's old polka-dot sheets hung limply on their nails.

I put the salt and pepper shakers back in the exact middle of the table and went outside. Sally was still next to the meander.

Sally is right. Lists go only so far.

Take Sally herself, in simple list form.

Name: Sally Wilmarth Hobart.
Nickname: None.
Home: North Sterns, New York, in the foothills of the Adirondack Mountains.
Family: Grandmother, Willie. Mother, Jill.
Grade: Passed sixth, heading into seventh.
Pets: None.
Favorite season: Spring.
Favorite color: White.
Best friend: Eddie Beckey.

Would someone reading this list know Sally? As an outline, maybe. But a chalk outline of a person is not a person. Nothing is filled in.

Looking at the pets category, someone might think that Sally doesn't care about pets. That person reading the list would not be able to picture Sally stroking Hedgy, the way she used to keep her fingers gentle and light so as not to hurt him.

That person would have no idea how much Sally wants a dog, no idea that she used to have an imaginary dog named Roscoe, an imaginary dog that she used to lead around with her jump rope as its leash.

Someone looking at the favorite-color category might think that white is a boring color to choose.

That person would have no idea that Sally's favorite color is white because it's all the colors of the spectrum in one. If you choose white, you're choosing every single color that exists in the entire world. Sally knows that, but how many other people do?

Someone looking at the family part of the

Sally list might think it unusual to list "Grandmother" before "Mother" and not to list "Father" at all.

That person would not know that Jill doesn't talk and that Sally has never lived with her. That person would not know about Willie and her green pail and her keep-away-the-dogs stick. That person would not know that Willie was an anti-sugarist or that Sally has vowed never again to eat another chocolate-covered sprinkle doughnut.

Looking at the list, no one would be able to tell that Willie is sick, that Willie will die soon.

I went outside, to where Sally was sitting beside the meander. I knelt beside her and combed my fingers through her hair, trying to bring some order to the tangles, trying to smooth some of the snarls.

"Sal, where does Nine Mile Creek go after it hits the Utica floodplain?" I said. "Have you ever found out?"

She shook her head.

"Do you think it might flow into the ocean eventually?"

No answer. I pictured the meander, flowing into Nine Mile Creek and then into the Utica floodplain and from there into a nameless river that grows bigger and bigger until it joins the Atlantic.

"The ocean refuses no river," Mr. Tyler told us in earth science.

"Sally," I said. "I'm so sorry."

I closed my eyes and laid my cheek against Sally's hair, her soft hair.

Her shoulders shook then, and I knew she was crying.

"It's hard, isn't it?" I whispered. "It's so hard, sometimes."

Twenty-two

It was quiet.

The last of the sun slipped behind the hills.

Darkness was nigh upon us and the Cabin started to become a dark shape, the way it always does at twilight, a shape without form, unrecognizable unless you had been camping there for many years and were used to it.

I closed my eyes and thought of the sound of Jill's voice.

*   *   *

To braid a braid:
1. Brush hair until smooth and snarl free.
2. Separate into three strands of equal size.
3. Hold all three strands loosely in both hands.
4. Draw one of the side strands over the middle strand, then draw the other side strand over the middle strand.
5. Pull tight for a tight braid, loose for a loose braid.
6. Keep drawing the sides over the middle until you have braided the length of the hair.

A slender pointed twig lay on the ground, and I used it to section Sally's hair. I made six braids, long ones that curved down her head and lay against the nape of her neck.

It took me a long time. I'm not used to braiding. I tied them with long strips of dried grass. Dried-grass bows.

When I was finished braiding Sally's hair, the braids I had made weren't even, not one exactly the same size and length as the others, nor were they made with clean parts, the kind you make with a comb. They were long and straggly. I saw that they wouldn't last. Already one of the dried-grass bows had slipped off. Tiny strands of hair were slipping away from the other strands. They were still braids, but they were braids unbraiding, turning into loose strands of hair.

I took the red rubber band off my wrist and wrapped it around the end of the longest braid. Then I took off the blue one, and the yellow, the white, and the pink.

The directions for how to braid make it seem as if there is one stationary middle strand, while the side strands are in constant motion, crossing over and over. But the reality is that there is no middle strand, nor are there side strands. The sides become the middle become the sides again in a braid. Each has equal weight. Each is always in motion. At any given moment, a side or a middle is in the process of becoming what it used to be and will be again.

The day will come that Sally and I will be all grown-up. Someday the Cabin will be fallen into the ground, taking with it our curtains, and the salt and pepper shakers that Sophie gave us that day. The meander will finally tire of its curves, and each curve will break through its wall of earth so that it is no longer a meander but a single straight thread of creek.

I have been growing my hair out since last Thanksgiving, and still no one has noticed. Maybe the day will come when I will be able to toss my head in exasperation, and someone will say, "Oh, you're growing out your bangs?" and I will sigh and say, "Yes." I believe that the day will come when Jill will say something for all to hear. I believe that there will come a day when Jill will know how to do Sally's hair, and Sally will get on the bus with her hair in a French braid that wraps itself around her head.

But for now, there was one more braid still undone.

I looked at my wrist and the single rubber band that remained.

If you are afraid, here's something you can try. Put a purple rubber band around your wrist, a rubber band that means "Be of strong heart." Snap it every day, whenever you are afraid, whenever you sense the world around you changing and you are scared of what may happen, and maybe someday you will have a glimpse of what it means to be brave.

Sally's head was still bent, and her shoulders curved with tiredness. Her eyes were closed. With a single finger I plucked the purple rubber band on my wrist as if it were a guitar string, so gently that it made no sound.

I slipped it off.

Then I wrapped it around Sally's shining hair, so that the last braid was held firmly in place.

ACKNOWLEDGMENTS

Thank you, Kara "editor extraordinaire" LaReau, for your encouragement and your keen eye.

Thank you, Mike Finley, for the blue bicycle, and thank you, Susan Andress, for the doughnut holes.

To the members of the Lake Harriet Community School Rope Power team and their teachers, a big cancan to you all!

And to Kate DiCamillo and Holly McGhee, first readers and editors, my love and thanks.

ALMOST HOME
Nora Raleigh Baskin

"I should have known something was wrong."

"Where's mum?"

"It wasn't your fault."

"I hate you!"

Leah Baer misses her mum; she writes to her almost every day. About not liking school. About Dad and Gail. And now about Will. But there is something that Leah doesn't mention to her mum in her letters, or even admit to herself. And until she does, Leah can't move on…

BECAUSE OF WINN-DIXIE
Kate DiCamillo

One summer's day, ten-year-old India Opal Buloni goes down to the local supermarket for some groceries – and comes home with a dog.

Winn-Dixie is no ordinary dog. Big, skinny and smelly he may be, but he also has the most winning smile. It's because of Winn-Dixie that Opal gets to know some very surprising people and starts to make new friends. It's because of Winn-Dixie that she finally dares to ask her father about her mother, who left when Opal was three.

In fact, just about everything that happens that summer is because of Winn-Dixie.

Read about the exploits of this most unusual dog and a host of quirky characters in this enchanting tale.

DOVEY COE
Frances O'Roark Dowell

"*My name is Dovey Coe and I reckon it don't matter if you like me or not. I'm here to lay the record straight, to let you know them folks saying I done a terrible thing are liars. I aim to prove it, too. I hated Parnell Caraway as much as the next person, but I didn't kill him.*"

Dovey Coe likes to speak her mind. She tells her beautiful older sister Caroline just what she thinks about no-good rich boy Parnell Caraway hanging round their house all summer. And she's quick to speak up for her deaf brother Amos when folks treat him like he's slow. But sometimes, speaking your mind can get you in a whole lot of trouble – as Dovey Coe discovers. Accused of murder, who will speak up for her?

Winner of the Mystery Writers of America's Edgar Award